DANGER MONEY

Mary Chapman

Evans

For Martin, with love

Published by Evans Brothers Limited
2A Portman Mansions
Chiltern St
London W1U 6NR

First published in 2007

British Library Cataloguing in Publication Data
Chapman, Mary
Danger Money. - (Shades)
1. Young adult fiction
I. Title
823. 9'2 [J]

ISBN 0 237 53202 6
13-digit ISBN 978 0 237 53202 4

Series Editor: David Orme
Editor: Julia Moffatt
Designer: Rob Walster

Chapter One

'Look out, Jim!' shouted Bob.

Baskets, piled with fish, swung over their heads from the fishing smack moored alongside the lower landing. The boys darted over the slippery wet stones, ducking their heads, grabbing the small silvery herrings that fell out of the basket, stuffing them into the bag they carried between them.

'That's full enough now,' said Bob. 'We'll get threepence at least from old Sam. Come on, Jim! We've got to get there first.'

Sam sold fish to the very poorest of the poor in Eastcliff. He bought it as cheaply as he could, and struck a hard bargain.

Pushing their way through the noisy crowded fish market they hurried from the harbour. The bag of fish bounced back and forth between them as they ran. By the time they turned down the narrow passage that led to Sam's small, dark shop Jim was gasping for breath.

'Only tuppence!' grumbled Bob as they came out of the shop.

He removed his left boot, carefully placed the two pennies inside and then put his boot back on again.

'What are we gonna do?' asked Jim. 'We can't go home with just tuppence. Whatever'll our Mam say?'

'I know,' said Bob. 'We'll go up the Tower. Come on, Jim.'

Back at the harbour they made their way to the old wooden coastguard lookout tower, known to everyone as the Tower, and ran up the wooden steps to the top. From there they could see right out to the cold grey North Sea.

At first they saw only a dark smudge in the distance, but as it came nearer they could make out its shape more clearly.

'It's got a long mizzen gaff,' said Bob.

'And patches on the mizzen,' added Jim.

'I can see the number now,' said Bob. '*EF 217*! It's the *Hilda Rose*. Fred Hudson from Chapel Lane's on that.'

'Let's go tell his missus,' said Jim.

They pounded down the stairs, raced along the jetty to Chapel Lane, and knocked on the front door of the first cottage in the row.

'Missus, come quick!' shouted Bob. 'Your husband's comin' in.'

Mrs Hudson opened the door.

'We seen the *Hilda Rose*,' gasped Jim. 'We've bin up on the Tower.'

'We've come straight here,' said Bob.

'Just a minute,' said Mrs Hudson. 'I'll get my purse.'

Bob and Jim grinned at each other.

'That's for you boys for runnin' up,' said Mrs Hudson, handing a penny to Bob.

'Mam'll be pleased,' said Jim. 'We've got threepence now.'

'Let's go back to the Tower,' said Bob, 'and see if we can make it fourpence.'

At the Tower two fishermen were standing at the bottom of the stairs. They were smartly dressed in warm overcoats and soft leather high heel boots. One of them even had a velvet collar to his coat, and gold rings in his ears. A gold ring gleamed on the little finger of his left hand.

As Bob and Jim squeezed past them the man with the ring spoke.

'I don't know what we're goin' to do, Alf, now Wilf's laid up. We're due to sail day after tomorrow.'

'I don't know of any young lads who'd do it at this short notice, Skipper,' said Alf.

'Do what?' asked Bob.

Skipper and Alf looked down at him.

'Not anything you could do, shrimp,' said Alf. 'We need a cook for the *Admiral*.'

'I can cook,' said Bob.

Jim opened his mouth but, at a look from Bob, closed it again.

'Been to sea before?' asked Alf.

'No, not yet, but my dad and grandad were fishermen.'

'Name?'

'My dad was Harry Thompson, from Denefield village, and Grandad was Arthur.'

'Good old fishing family,' said Skipper. 'How old are you, lad?'

'Fifteen-and-a-half,' said Bob.

'Hmm. Small for your age. You're old enough, but are you big enough?' asked Alf.

Bob tried to stand taller.

'What about yer mam?' asked Skipper. 'Weren't it only two year ago she lost your dad? End of nineteen-fourteen, just after war started?'

'Yes,' said Bob.

'You the eldest?' asked Alf.

'Yes, but our Lizzie's at home. She's fourteen and Jim here, he's thirteen. You and Lizzie'll look after our Mam and the littl'uns, won't yer, Jim?'

'Aye, we will,' said Jim confidently.

'Now you're sure you can cook?' asked Skipper. 'There'll be nine of us.'

Bob gave Jim a warning look, and nodded.

'Well, we'll give you a try,' said Skipper. 'Beggars can't be choosers. You'll need the proper gear – oilskin, boots, the lot. Can you manage that?'

'Mam's still got our Dad's stuff,' said Bob. 'I can wear that.'

'The *Admiral*'s an armed smack,' said Skipper. 'That means you get two shillings a day extra – danger money. That's five and six a day all told.'

Bob's eyes widened.

'I'll do it,' Bob said. 'I'll go home now an' get my stuff.'

'Right then,' said Skipper. 'An' call on old Joe Tate at Arbour Farm on your way back to Denefield, an' ask him if you can have a sack to fill with straw. An' mind you fill it as tight as you can, 'cos that'll be your bed, lad. Make sure you bring it with you Wednesday mornin'. Be here first light or we'll go without you.'

'I'll be there!' said Bob.

'Mind you are,' said Alf.

Chapter Two

'You can 'ave this sack. It's nice an' dry,' said
Joe Tate. 'Stuff the straw in as tight as you
can – tight as a drum. It'll last you a twelve-
month then, an' you'll sleep like a babby.'

Bob and Jim knelt on the floor of the dim
dusty barn. Jim held the sack open while
Bob gathered armfuls of wheat straw and
pushed it down into the sack.

'What's yer mam goin' to say to this?' asked Joe.

Bob shrugged.

'Well, it's in yer blood,' said Joe, 'but it's dangerous work. Them German submarines, them U-boats – they'll be out to get you.'

'I'll be all right,' said Bob, 'and it's good money – two bob extra a day.'

'You'll earn it, lad,' said Joe.

'Mam! Mam! Our Bob's goin' in the *Admiral*!' shouted Jim, suddenly dropping his end of the sack of straw and running ahead of Bob.

Bob hoisted the sack onto his shoulder and hurried after his brother. But it was too late. By the time he'd dropped the sack onto the floor just inside the back door, Jim had told their mother everything.

She stood, wiping her hands on her pinafore. 'What's all this, Bob?' she asked quietly.

Bob didn't answer. He took the three pennies out of his boot and put them on the table.

'Bob?'

'We got tuppence from old Sam, and Mrs Hudson gave us a penny for runnin' up. The *Hilda Rose* come in.'

His mother didn't even glance at the money.

'Never mind the *Hilda Rose*. What's this about the *Admiral*?'

'I'm goin' as cook. It's two bob a day extra. So that'll be five an' six a day, an' my grub included. We go Wednesday.'

His mother pulled a chair out from the table and sat down.

'Why d'you think they pay two bob a day extra?'

Bob stared at the three pennies.

His mother shook her head. 'To get you to

risk your life, son. It's not worth it. I lost your dad to the sea. I don't want to lose you.'

'Joe Tate says it's in my blood,' said Bob.

'It's all very well for Joe Tate. He's got a farm. His sons'll never have to go to sea. We can manage as we are.'

'We can't, Mam. Land work doesn't pay. I've been stood off months on end. We could just about manage when Dad was alive, but not now. I want to go to sea. I'm a Thompson.'

'Mam!' shouted Jim. 'Somethin's burnin'.'

Smoke was rising from a heavy black iron pot on the kitchen range.

'Oh, no! It's the dinner!'

She jumped up and lifted the lid. The smell of burnt potatoes and turnips wafted into the room.

'Look what you've made me go an' do!' she snapped.

Bob looked down at his boots.

His mother sighed. 'We'll talk about it after dinner.' And she turned away.

'Come on, Jim,' said Bob. He opened the door beside the range. Jim followed him up the winding stairs that led directly into their mother's room. Under the window was an old brown tin trunk. Bob lifted the lid. There was a damp, musty smell. He took out a pair of duffle trousers, and held them up against himself. They were far too long.

'Bob, you'd best put 'em back,' said Jim. 'You should ask our Mam first.'

Bob dropped the trousers on to the floor, and delved into the trunk. There was an oilskin, a brownish calico jumper, a flannel shirt, knitted boot stockings, a bundle of strips of red flannel and, at the bottom, a pair of long boots.

'Jim! Bob! What are you doin' up there?

Come down for your dinners!'

Bob tumbled everything back into the trunk, and quietly closed the lid.

'I'm goin' on Wednesday, Jim. No matter what our Mam says.'

Chapter Three

Bob stood in front of the kitchen range, eating the bread and dripping his mother had cut. She'd got up as soon as she heard him moving about. It was still dark outside.

His little sister Evie had come downstairs when she heard voices. She sat on the old sofa, wrapped in her mother's shawl. The door at the bottom of the stairs opened, and

Lizzie tiptoed into the room.

'Shall I wake the boys, Mam?'

'No. Let 'em sleep.'

'But, Mam, they'll want to say goodbye.'

'No!' Her mother's voice was sharp.
'There's no need to make a song an' dance
about it. He'll be back in a few days. They
need their rest. They're stone picking on
Newton Beach today.'

Puzzled, Lizzie went and sat by Evie. Bob
quickly swallowed the last of his bread and
dripping.

Evie jumped off the sofa.

'I want to go down the harbour with Bob.'

'No, Evie,' said her mother. 'We're not
going to see Bob off. It's bad luck.'

Evie ran to Bob and grabbed his hand.
'But I wanna go with Bob.'

'No, Evie, an' that's the end of it.'

Evie clung to Bob, but her mother pulled

her away. Evie began to cry.

'I'm goin' now,' said Bob. The room had gone all blurry.

His mother pressed two pennies into his hand.

'For luck,' she said.

Bob hoisted the sack of straw onto his back, opened the door and went out into the cold dawn.

The harbour was busy with men and boys hurrying to their boats. Bob threaded his way through the crowd.

'There's the *Admiral*,' someone said. 'They say she's just had a thirteen-pounder fitted.'

'She'll need it,' said another man. 'She sunk a sub when she'd only been out two days, so them subs'll be after her. She only had a five-pounder then.'

Both men laughed. Bob felt excited and

scared. He knew what they were talking about. All the armed sailing smacks had a gun on deck to defend themselves. A thirteen-pounder was really big.

Down the fish market he'd heard men talk about the *Admiral's* maiden trip as an armed smack. Except she was the *Victoria* then. They changed the boats' names to try to confuse the enemy. But whatever the name, male or female, a boat was always a 'she'. His dad told him that when he was only a bairn.

'Hurry up, lad. There's no time for gawping!'

It was Alf.

'Come on. Follow me, and make sharp about it.'

He took Bob down into the cabin.

'Now you know who's Skipper,' he said, 'and I'm Mate, next in charge. You're ninth man so you take notice of what I say. Put your sack down there. It's a bit cramped 'cos there's only five bunks for the nine of us.'

'Why's that?' asked Bob.

'The gunners and the chap who looks after the motor,' said Alf. 'They're extra – volunteers from the Navy. 'Course they're not wearin' their uniforms. Don't want to give it away to Jerry, do we? Let him think we're just simple fishermen. Then give him a surprise!'

He laughed. Bob laughed too, though he wasn't sure it was very funny.

'I'll get George now,' said Alf. 'He's third hand. He'll show you the galley, and where the grub is, and the pots and pans.'

'All the grub's in these lockers,' said George. 'There's plenty o' flour. We're partial to dumplings with our stew, or a nice beef puddin'. An' here's a sack o' sea biscuits. They're hard as iron, but soak 'em in sea water an' then stick 'em in the oven. Lovely!'

He opened the sack.

'Ugh!' said Bob. 'What's them?'

Little gold and silver insects darted amongst the biscuits.

'They're only little ol' weevils,' said George. 'If they don't drown when you soak 'em, they'll burn to death when you put 'em in the oven. 'Course there'll be plenty o' fish, for breakfast, dinner and tea! That'll keep you busy!'

Bob swallowed nervously.

'You can cook, lad, can't you?'

'Yeah … I just haven't cooked for nine before, on a boat,' said Bob.

'It's all right, mate. Me and deckie'll help you to start with. I'll give him a shout.'

Chapter Four

With the help of George and Tom, the deckhand, Bob started getting dinner ready. The meat went into a big roasting tin, and then into the coal-fired oven. George told him when to add water, potatoes, and finally cabbage. Everything went into the one tin.

'D'ye know how to make a light duff?' asked Tom. 'Dumplings?'

Bob shook his head. The movement of the boat had changed. It was more of a rolling motion. He felt strange.

'Are you feeling qualmy?' asked Tom. 'Y'know, sea-sick?'

'I dunno. Maybe.'

'All the best sailors are sea-sick first time out,' said Tom cheerfully. 'Just don't eat any dinner or tea today and you'll be all right for the rest of the trip. Now I'll show you how to make a lovely light duff. I was cook on my first trip, on the *Swan*. I didn't know anything about cookin', just like you! Sid Ward showed me, so I'll show you.'

Bob watched Tom as he deftly made dumplings, and added them to the stew. He felt hot and faint. He tried to think about that extra two shillings a day, imagining himself going home and putting the money on the table, money he'd earned. He wished he was home now, instead of sailing out into the middle of the North Sea.

While the others ate their dinner Bob lay down, on deck. Gradually he started to feel better, and sat up and looked around. Right next to him was a bulky object, covered over by a tarpaulin. He leaned over and lifted the corner of the tarpaulin.

'Hey, you. Leave that be!'

It was Bert, one of the gunners.

'I was only lookin', I wasn't goin' to touch it,' said Bob.

'Mind you don't,' said Bert.

'When'll you fire it?' asked Bob.

'When Jerry gets too close,' said Bert. 'The gun's hidden so Jerry thinks we're an ordinary fishing smack. He comes alongside, all ready to sink us, but we fire on him, an' he sinks instead.'

'Are there any submarines out there

now?' asked Bob.

'No,' said Bert, 'but you have to keep your eyes skinned all the time. He's cunning is Jerry.'

Bob stood by the gun for a long time, straining his eyes as he searched the horizon.

'See them gulls divin',' said Tom, coming to stand beside him. 'They know there's herring thereabouts, an' there's a good sou'west breeze. It's time to shoot the nets, an' catch them herrings.'

Alf joined them.

'Bob, there's a job for you, down below.'

Bob still felt a bit qualmy, but he didn't want Skipper or Alf wishing they hadn't taken him on. He followed Alf down the ladder.

'When we're hauling the nets,' said Alf, 'your job is to coil the trawl warp, like this, real neat, round the capstan. You have to make sure this old rope don't twist as you wind it.'

'I can do that,' said Bob.

'It's not as easy as it looks,' said Alf. 'You're only a little 'un.'

'I'm strong,' said Bob.

'We'll see,' said Alf.

Suddenly they heard Skipper's voice, louder even than usual, booming out,

'In the name o' the Lord, pay away!'

'There they go,' said Alf. 'Now listen hard, young Bob. After we've shot the trawl, and Skipper thinks we've towed long enough, you'll hear him holler, "Haul King George's trawl!" You got that?'

'Yes,' said Bob.

'That's when you start a-coiling the trawl warp,' said Alf.

'Have you got some red flannel bandages with your gear?' Tom asked, coming down the hatchway.

Bob nodded.

'Then soak some of 'em in paraffin, an' wrap 'em round your wrists,' advised Tom. 'That'll stop 'em from chafing.'

But it didn't, not after coiling the warp hour after hour, round and round. The rope was as thick as Bob's fist. It hurt his hands so they were sore and burning. Water ran off the rope into the sleeves of his oilskin and down his arms. He felt qualmy again, but he had to keep going, round and round, making sure the rope was coiled neat and tidy.

It was dark now, and they couldn't show any lights in case the enemy saw them. He was so tired. His arms and legs ached. At home he'd be asleep now, in a soft warm feather bed, Jim snoring beside him, Ted and Dave in the other bed, Mam, Lizzie and Evie in the next room.

The cold was making his eyes water.

Chapter Five

It was the third day of Bob's first trip.
They'd just finished dinner – meat, spuds,
turnips and dumplings. Bob washed up the
plates, pots and pans, and scrubbed the
table. He put some sea biscuits to soak in a
bowl of cold water. Later he'd stick them in
a tin in the oven, so they'd be hot and
toasty for tea. The men loved them.

The wind had dropped, so Skipper started up the little petrol engine. Bob could hear its gentle throbbing.

Suddenly there was another sound, one he'd never heard before.

Dududududu … dududududu … dudu dududu … dududududududududu…

Bert, who was on deck, shouted down to the cabin, to the other gunners.

'Ernie! Ned! Arthur!'

They were up off their bunks in a moment.

Dududududu … dududududu … dudududu … dududududududududu…

Bob stood by the table, unable to move. Above him feet pounded across the deck. He could hear the men cursing and shouting to each other.

'They've hit the *Triton*!'

'I can't see Jerry. He's gone down.'

'There he is. He's comin' straight for us!'

'Let 'im 'ave it!'

An explosion of noise.

Now he understood why he got two shillings a day danger money.

The *Admiral* shook with the vibration. Pots and pans clattered. Bob made a grab for the biscuits, but the bowl slipped out of his grasp and slid on to the floor.

Tom came down.

'It's all right, boy,' he said. 'We got 'im. He come straight up out o' the water, an' he were comin' straight for us, an' our shell hit his connin' tower. Come an' see. There's oil all over the water.'

Bob followed Tom slowly up on to the deck. There was no sign of the submarine, but a layer of thick black oil was spreading all over the water.

It was very quiet now. The only noise was the sound of the engine.

'Better put the dan overboard, Tom,' said Skipper, 'to show where the sub went down.'

Tom slid the long, thin buoy overboard. It bobbed about in the oily water, its small flag fluttering.

'We'll make for home now,' said the Skipper. 'Go and get the tea on, lad.'

After tea, Bob went up on deck. There on the starboard side, steaming towards them was a huge boat, frothing at the bows. Bob felt his stomach churn.

'What's that? Is it Jerry?' he asked Ned the gunner, who was on watch.

'No, one of ours,' replied Ned. 'Navy frigate, one of them P-boats, chases subs.'

The frigate came closer. They could see the captain on his bridge.

'Where's the sub, Skipper?' he shouted through his megaphone.

'We've sunk him!' shouted Skipper.

The captain turned to the sailors on the frigate.

'Three cheers for the old Eastcliff smack!' he shouted.

'Hip! Hip! Hooray! Hip! Hip! Hooray! Hip! Hip! Hooray!'

Their voices rang out over the cold grey sea.

Bob felt like a hero.

Chapter Six

Bob soon forgot how scared he'd been when the submarine attacked them. He just remembered how proud he felt when the sailors cheered, and when crowds turned out to welcome the *Admiral* back to Eastcliff. He'd had extra leave, ten days, survivors' leave they called it. He was happy to be home, but when his leave ended he was ready to return to sea.

That's how it continued for the next few months, with neither sight nor sound of a German sub. At sea for five or six days, then home for two or three. As time went by, and he returned safe and sound from every trip, his mam seemed more content. She was proud of her fisherman son. Maybe one day he'd be deckie, then third hand, then mate, and even, one day, Skipper. His mam did his washing. Lizzie and Eve fussed round him. Jim, Ted and Dave loved to hear the story, over and over again, of how the *Admiral* had sunk a Jerry sub. It was a hard life, but a good one. At the end of every trip he felt so pleased when he handed over his pay to his mam.

The extra two bob a day towered up. One day Mam said, 'You can go down to Perry, and get some new trousers for best, and a jersey and a warm coat.'

Bob went into Eastcliff and bought trousers, a jersey and a fine overcoat.

'And I'll have that wrapper, please,' he said to Mr Perry, the men's outfitter, pointing to a handsome silk neckerchief. Mam hadn't said he could, but he was sure she wouldn't mind. He'd look so grand.

His long sea-boots needed mending, so he took them to Harry Foster, the bootmaker, near the harbour, who repaired all the fishermen's boots.

'You'll have to leave 'em here,' said Harry. 'I'll have 'em ready for your next shore leave.'

Bob looked along the shelves. He noticed a row of high-heeled boots, made of softest leather. On each toe-cap there was a pattern of an anchor or a heart. He must have a pair.

'It's all right then, is it?' asked Harry, as he counted out the coins Bob handed over. 'Worth the danger money, is it?'

'We've not seen a sub for six months now,' said Bob. 'It's money for jam!'

Leaving the shop, he set off along the street, looking down at his feet to admire his new boots, each gleaming toe-cap adorned with an anchor. He walked with a swagger, just like all the fishermen did when they were on shore.

'Money for jam!' he said to himself.

Chapter Seven

Early one hot Wednesday afternoon in August Bob was on deck, cleaning the fish for next morning's breakfast. It was a messy job, scraping the scales of the herring, then splitting them and removing the innards. Gulls swooped overhead, then dived down for the guts as Bob threw them overboard. Because of the gulls' screeching he didn't hear Skipper come up behind him.

'Bob,' said Skipper, 'just get me the glasses.'

Bob got up off his knees, rubbing his hands on his trousers. He fetched the glasses off the mizzenmast, and handed them to Skipper who was staring intently to starboard.

'There's a couple of submarines out there,' Skipper said.

Bob stared in the same direction. He wasn't sure if he could see something, or if he was imagining it.

'Yes, there's definitely two of 'em,' said Skipper. 'Go an' tell everybody to be ready for action.'

Bob's heart pounded in his chest. *Two* submarines against one little fishing smack. He ran to tell the others. Then he went to his own action station, with George, down below in the fore-peak, in the ammunition room.

'Take them shells out of their boxes,' said George, 'and hand 'em to me so's I can hook 'em on to these ropes. Bert and Ernie'll pull the ropes up an' unhook the shells an' Ned'll load 'em into the gun. There's no time to lose.'

Bob was all fingers and thumbs. He tried to be as quick as he could. George was swearing under his breath. The gunners were shouting to each other. Before they could fire a shell the submarine opened fire on the *Admiral*.

There was a tremendous explosion, followed straightaway by another, even louder. Bob was sure they'd been hit. His ears rang and his hands trembled.

'It's all right,' said George. 'We've not been hit. Pass us another boxful.'

Their own gunners retaliated. The whole boat vibrated, just as it had when they sank that Jerry submarine a few months ago. It seemed so easy then. One shot, and it went down. Not this time. Their shots were falling short. The sub was keeping its distance.

Another explosion, and another. The *Admiral's* gunners fired back again. There was a tremendous reverberation throughout the boat, and the smell of smoke.

Another explosion. Really close. A flash. The boat shuddered. Bob heard water splashing.

Then he heard Alf shout,

'He's hit us on the starboard bow!'

'A little further for'ard, an' we'd both have bin gonners,' said George.

Bob felt sick. He longed to be in the fresh air. It was hot and cramped in the ammo room, but he had to stay and do his bit. The terrible noise, the ringing in his ears, the stench of gunfire. What if the boat went down, and he and George were trapped?

His knees hurt with crouching down by the boxes of shells. He stood up to stretch his legs.

'All right?' asked George.

'Yes,' said Bob, though he wasn't. He was more scared than he'd ever been. What had he said to Harry Foster? Money for jam. Tempting providence, that's what Mam would call it. He wished he'd never said it.

'My ears are ringin' that bad I can't hear a thing,' said George. 'Just go an' find out what's goin' on. Don't put your head above deck though.'

'He's out of range,' Bob heard Arthur shout.

'Hang fire for a bit,' called Skipper. 'Wait

'til they come nearer an' then give 'em another blast.'

Crack! Another shell came over. And another. A hit. The boat shook.

The *Admiral's* gunners fired back, but they couldn't hit Jerry. He was too far off.

There was another bang, quickly followed by another, and a terrible juddering.

'It's gone through the mainsail!' yelled Alf. 'Oh, God, that one's gone right through the port quarter!'

'Abandon ship!' shouted Skipper.

Bob ran back to George. Skipper was right behind him.

'We're sinkin' fast,' Skipper said. 'Come on!'

On deck Alf, Tom and Bert were unfastening the little boat, ready to launch it. Smoke swirled around them.

Bob felt the salt water spray on his face.

He could taste it. Water!

He kicked off his boots, his beautiful new boots. There was no point in wearing them. The high heels would be a nuisance. They'd have to go down with the ship.

He turned and raced down below. Water was coming in so fast it was nearly up to his knees. Where was the old tea-kettle? Here! He managed to fill it with fresh water.

Back on deck Skipper was taking the carrier pigeon, Red Runner, out of its coop.

'Hold him, Bob,' he said, 'while I write a message.'

Bob watched as he wrote, 'Armed smack the *Admiral* attacked by submarine – Hardy Shoal Buoy.'

While Bob held the pigeon steady, Skipper stuffed the rolled-up paper through the ring on its leg. Then he held it aloft and let it go.

Skipper and Alf lifted the big compass out of the *Admiral*, and passed it down to George and Tom in the little boat. Once they were all aboard they pulled clear of the *Admiral* as fast as they could. She was going down. They didn't want the little boat, their only hope of survival, to be dragged down with her.

When they were at a safe enough distance they rested the oars, and watched in silence as the *Admiral* tilted and disappeared beneath the waves.

Chapter Eight

The little boat was only built for five, so it was very cramped.

'One of us'll have to bale out all the time,' said Skipper. 'She's leakin' like anythin', even though Bob's a littl 'un, and don't weigh much.'

Bob had always wished he was bigger, but now he was glad he was small.

'We'll take it in turns to row while the others try an' get a bit o' sleep,' continued Skipper. 'We'll go eastwards first. Try an' throw Jerry off our trail.'

'Compass ain't workin' right,' said Alf. 'It's swingin' about all over the place. This ol' boat's jerkin' about too much.'

Skipper cursed.

'We'll have to do the best we can. Sail by the Pole Star at night, an' the sun by day.'

Bob was afraid the boat would capsize. It was so low in the water. If it did, that would be it. He couldn't swim. His dad had always said there was no point. If you went overboard in your oilskins and boots you'd sink like a stone anyway.

Just then the submarine fired at them again. A shell dropped, exploding in the water. The boat rocked violently. Ernie was baling out frantically. Skipper turned the boat in the other direction.

'Look over there,' said Alf. 'I reckon there's a sea mist coming up.'

'That'd be a bit o' luck,' said Arthur.

'It'd be a bloomin' miracle,' said Ernie.

Alf was right. The sun went hazy at first, and then disappeared. The air felt cooler, although it was only the middle of the afternoon. White mist swirled around them. Occasionally they caught a glimpse of the sub, but Jerry couldn't see them, hidden by the murky sea-fog.

The clammy vapour seeped through Bob's trousers. He shuddered.

'You have your turn at rowing now,' said George. 'That'll warm you up. Give me the old kettle. I'll hang on to that. It's the only fresh water we've got.'

'You did well to think of it, Bob,' said Skipper.

After he'd been rowing for a while Bob started to feel warmer. The mist lifted, and there was no sight of Jerry.

'What was that?' asked Ned.

They let the boat drift so they could listen.

'I reckon it's gunfire,' said Bert.

'Sounds like the *Triton*'s getting it,' said Skipper. 'We'll have to keep dodging about to stay out of Jerry's way.'

They were silent, thinking of those other fishermen. Quietly Bob and Tom started to row again.

About midnight Skipper said, 'I think we'll make for Eastcliff now.'

So they turned west.

Through the long night they took turns at rowing, and baling out. Every time they swapped over, they passed round the kettle, and took just one sip of water each. Bob's hands were blistered from the rowing. His arms and back ached. He was cold, wet and hungry.

Dawn came at last, the sky streaked with green and orange. A huge sun rose above the horizon. It was going to be a hot day. The sea was empty. No submarines, no fishing boats.

'Keep the sun to stern now,' said Skipper, 'an' as it gets higher in the sky we'll keep it to port, an' then sail due west into the sunset.'

All through the long hot day, in the blistering heat, while the sun shone down from a clear sky, they took it in turns to bale out water and to row. The hours rowing or baling seemed endless. The hours resting passed in a flash.

Bob's wrists were raw where the oilskin

rubbed, and his neck was sore too. His arms and shoulders ached from rowing. His legs ached as well. There wasn't enough room to stretch out. The heat made his bug-bites itch unbearably.

'There's some minesweepers out there, to starboard!' called George.

For a long time they all shouted and waved at the dark shapes in the distance. But instead of getting bigger, they got smaller, and finally disappeared below the horizon.

During their second night in the little boat, keeping the Pole Star to starboard, they moved slowly forward through the dark waves. The temperature dropped. At first Bob felt better, but then his feet, without boots, got colder and colder in their wet, woollen socks.

The screaming of the wind, and the rocking of the boat woke Bob at first light.

Grey clouds, grey sea. No horizon.

'We're in for a storm,' said Skipper.

It was time for Bob to take a turn at rowing. He tried not to think about anything, except pulling on the oars.

Then Alf, sitting in the bow, shouted out, 'Reckon I can see a buoy!'

'Could be Marshall Sand,' said Tom.

The thought of being nearly home made Bob row harder.

After a while Alf spoke again. This time his voice was flat.

'No, it's not Marshall Sand. It's the Hardy Shoal Buoy.'

'It can't be!' shouted Bert. 'D'ye mean to say we've bin pullin' an' pullin' two days an' two nights an' we're still in the same place?'

The men cursed and swore.

'An' where's that bloomin' pigeon got to?' asked Ernie.

'I reckon we should keep on rowin'
anyway,' said Arthur.

Ned and Bert nodded.

'Waste o' time in this storm,' said Tom.
'We'll wear ourselves out. We've no food.
There's hardly any water left. We'd best
make fast to the buoy.'

'At least get some rest from rowing,' said
George.

Skipper and Alf were talking quietly
together. Then Skipper spoke.

'More than anythin' we need rest. When
this wind blows itself out we'll get nearer to
the buoy an' tie the painter to it. The only
thing is, one of us is goin' to have to jump
aboard the buoy.'

Chapter Nine

It was a cage buoy. It used to have a bell to warn fishermen of rocks or shoals, but the bell was taken out so enemy ships wouldn't know they were in danger of running aground.

Who would be able to stay on there, hanging on to the uprights? Everyone's arms ached from rowing. They were weak from lack of food and water. There wasn't much of a foothold on the buoy. Although the wind had dropped, high waves were sloshing around it. The little boat felt steady and spacious in comparison.

Bob spoke out of the silence.

'I'll go, Skipper.'

'But you're tired, lad,' said Tom.

'I'm strong,' said Bob. 'Farm work gives you muscles.'

'Well,' said Skipper. 'You're light, an' you're wiry an' agile. But are you sure?'

'Yes,' said Bob, 'so long as I can borrow somebody's boots.'

They all managed to laugh.

'Good lad,' said Tom. 'Reckon I'm nearest your size. Have mine.'

When Bob had put on Tom's long sea-boots he stood up, balancing as best he could, ready to leap on to the buoy. Skipper was trying to get as close as possible, but there was a strong flood tide going against them.

'This is as near as we can get!' Skipper shouted. 'We'll throw the painter once you're on the buoy.'

Bob took a deep breath, put one foot on the edge of the boat, then the other and immediately launched himself across the gap between the boat and the buoy. He managed to get a foothold, and grabbed one of the uprights with one hand, and a vertical bar with the other. The metal was cold and slippery, but he held on.

'Well done!' shouted Skipper. 'Alf'll throw you the painter now. Ready?'

'Yes!' shouted Bob, clinging to the buoy.

Alf took the thick rope and threw it towards the buoy. It fell short, dropping into the water. The tide was so strong that the boat was moving away from the buoy.

'Pull, lads, pull!' shouted Skipper.

This time Alf managed to sling the rope so Bob could grab it with his right hand, holding on to the buoy with his left.

'Tie the rope round!' shouted Skipper.

Reaching round the buoy Bob felt his feet slipping. He stopped. There was no sound from the men in the boat. He could feel the rope pulling. There wasn't much slack. Maybe there wasn't enough rope to go round. It tightened, cutting into his hands. He mustn't let go.

The boat was behind him, so he couldn't see what was happening. Then the rope slackened. They must have got closer. He must tie the rope now, before the tide pulled the boat away again.

He'd done it. The rope was secure. And this was where he'd have to stay until they were rescued. Surely it'd be soon. The minute the pigeon had arrived back at Eastcliff they'd have sent out a boat...

Minutes, hours passed. After a while Bob couldn't feel his hands or his feet. But the cold didn't numb the pain of the salt-water boils on his neck and his wrists, or the stinging of salt water on his face.

He was dreaming, hearing voices: *dangerous work, lad … out to get you …* his mother's voice, *don't want to lose you …* the gleaming kitchen range; the smell of bread and dripping. He was so cold, men's voices from the little boat … opening his eyes, turning his head. It was such a little boat, so low in the water, in such a huge, empty sea. Nobody would find them. Everyone would think they'd gone down by now, drowned like his dad. And all for an extra two bob a day … *money for jam …* Mam was right. *It's not worth it.* Voices. Jim and Lizzie, Ted and Dave and little Evie … they were calling his name … *Bob! Bob!…*

'Bob!' shouted Skipper. 'Smoke!'

He opened his eyes, jerking awake. He was sliding. He'd almost fallen off. He grabbed the metal bars and heaved himself up.

'Over there!' shouted Alf.

'Warship,' said Skipper. 'Bert, you can semaphore. Send a signal quick. Tell 'em we're the crew of the *Admiral*.'

Bob was properly awake now. He twisted his head to watch the ship, as it steamed towards them. Would they see Bert's signal in time?

As the ship got closer Bob could see men leaning over the side. When would it be close enough for him to jump? His feet were so numb with cold he was afraid that if he moved he would just slither off the buoy and into the water. He would be sucked under the warship, and drown, exhausted and weak, weighed down by his oilskin and Tom's boots.

'Hang on, lad!' shouted a voice from the

warship. 'I'll tell you when to jump.'

Bob waited, his heart pounding.

'Now! Jump for it! Towards the bow!'

He jumped.

His foot caught in the loop of the anchor chain. He clutched the chain, hauling himself up. Hands reached down, grabbed at his clothing, dragged him up on deck.

When they were all aboard the warship, Bob learned just how much danger they'd been in, even at the very last minute when they were about to be rescued, and he'd thought they were safe at last.

'When we first saw you,' said the captain, 'we thought you were the sub. You looked such a strange shape – the boat hanging from the buoy. We couldn't really make it out. We were all ready to fire.'

Bert's semaphore signal had stopped them only just in time.

The warship took them as near shore as she could, dropped anchor and then signalled for a patrol boat to take them into Eastcliff.

The harbour was crowded with people who'd turned out to welcome them home. Bob knew that somewhere in the crowd would be Mam, Lizzie, Jim, Ted, Dave and little Evie. He couldn't wait to see them.

He imagined them, when they'd first heard about the *Admiral,* hurrying along the dusty lanes from Denefield to join the anxious crowd at the harbour. They'd have waited, full of dread, until they'd heard the crew was safe, and the news spread that a sharp-eyed lad, watching from the top of the Tower, had sighted the boat bringing the crew back to Eastcliff.

Bob didn't just feel like a hero. He *was* one. He'd earned his danger money.

Author's note

I was inspired to write *Danger Money* by reading *The Trawlermen,* a book about the East Anglian Fishing Industry, by David Butcher (Tops Books,1980). There I came across a young fisherman's eyewitness account of the sinking of the *Nelson,* an armed fishing boat from Lowestoft, Suffolk. This led me to visit the Lowestoft and East Suffolk Maritime Museum where I saw exhibits relating to the *Nelson,* including a local newspaper report and a model of the boat.

In the early years of World War I large numbers of British fishing boats were attacked and blown up by German submarines, so it was decided to equip some of them with guns. The crews of these armed boats were paid extra, 'danger money', because of the additional risks involved.

Danger Money, the story of the sinking of the *Admiral,* an armed fishing boat from Eastcliff, is loosely based on the accounts I have read of the sinking of the *Nelson*, although some events have been omitted or changed, and all the characters are imaginary.

Mary Chapman
March 2006